MY First
100
THINGS
that move

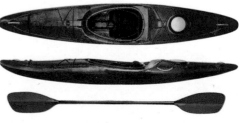

land transport

bicycle

scooter

motorcycle

car

van

bus

caravan

roller skates

skateboard

unicycle

stroller

go-kart

tandem

rickshaw

golf cart

handcar

snowmobile

fire engine

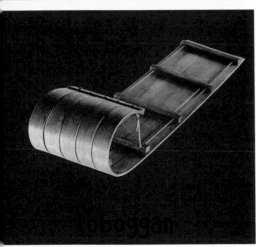

toboggan

quad bike

ambulance

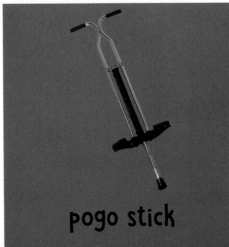

pogo stick

taxi

auto rickshaw

food wagon

monorail

tram

snow sled

garbage truck

tricycle

school bus

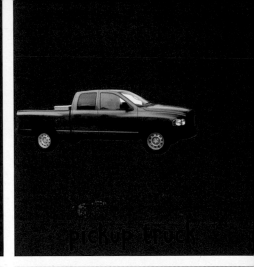

pickup truck

police car

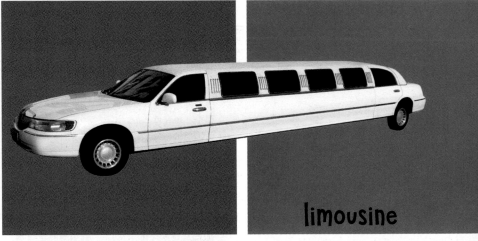

limousine

lorry

solar car

air transport

airplane

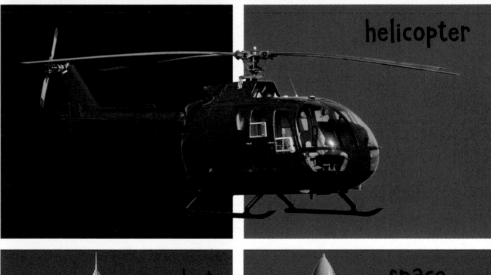

helicopter

rocket

space shuttle

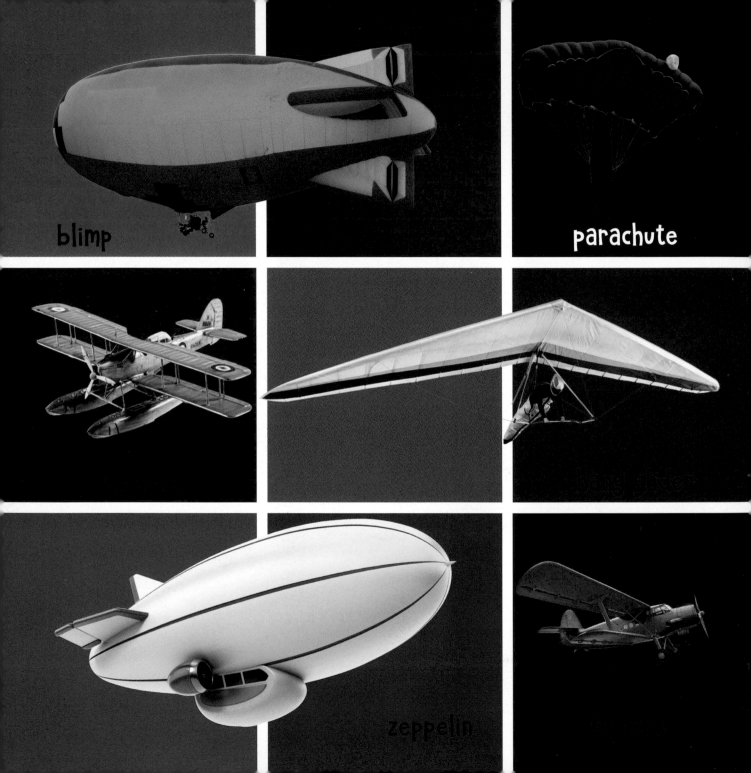

blimp

parachute

hang glider

zeppelin

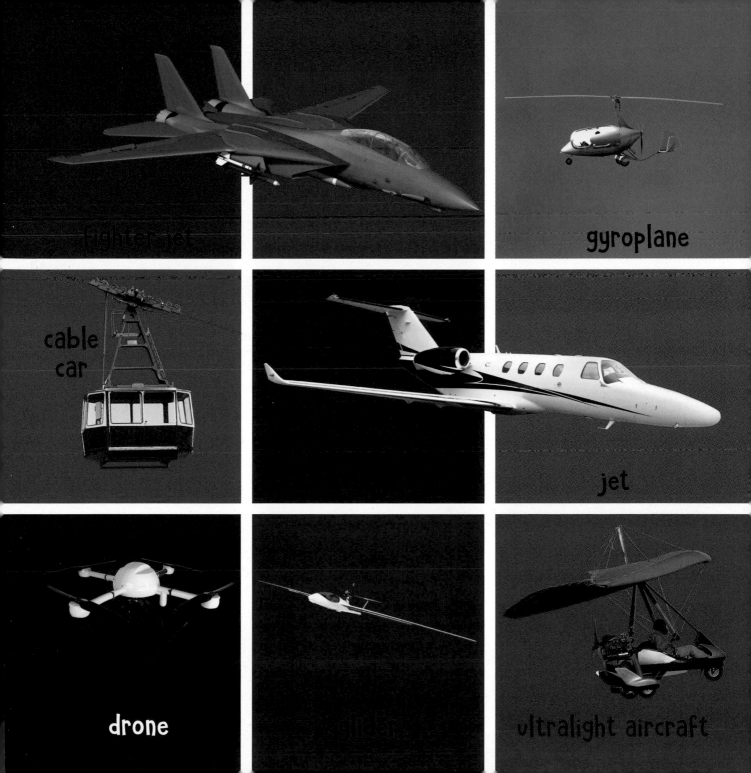

fighter jet

gyroplane

cable car

jet

drone

glider

ultralight aircraft

water transport

boat

motorboat

yacht

swan boat

cruise ship

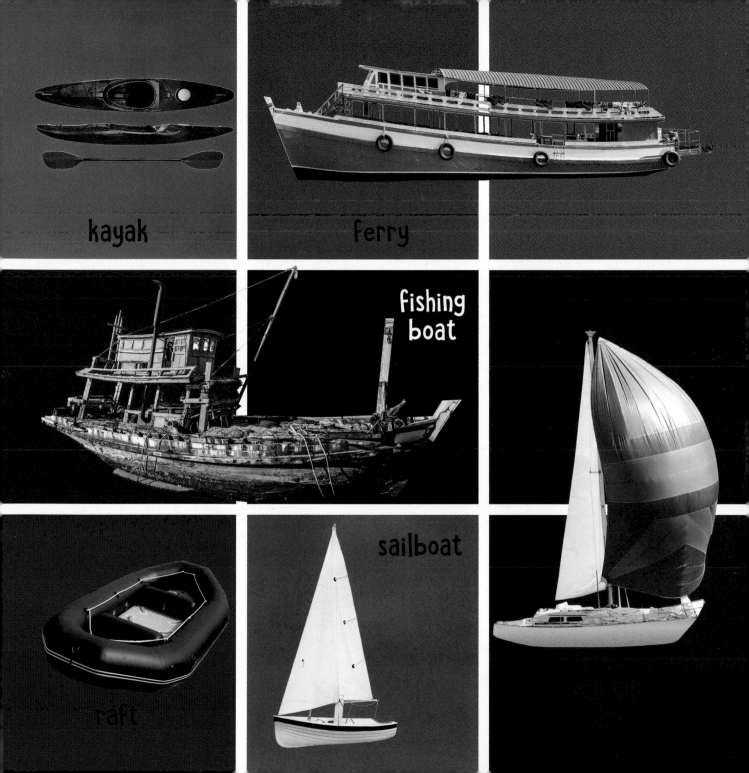

kayak

ferry

fishing boat

sailboat

raft

tugboat

frigate

555

hovercraft

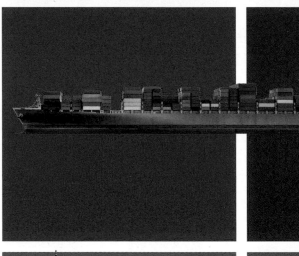

cargo ship

oil tanker

fireboat

canoe

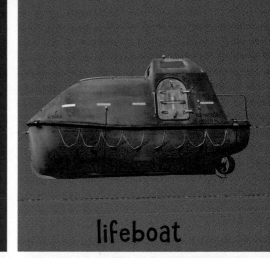

lifeboat

jet ski

surfboard

houseboat

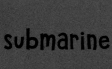

submarine

heavy transport

tow truck

road roller

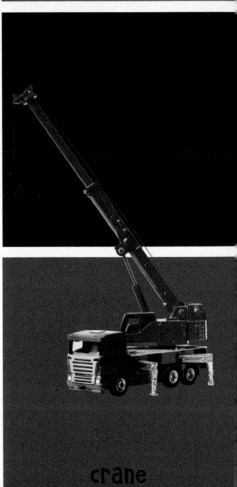

combine harvester

payloader

crane

tractor

cherry picker

bulldozer

concrete mixer truck

land grader

snowplow

hydraulic
hammer

harvester

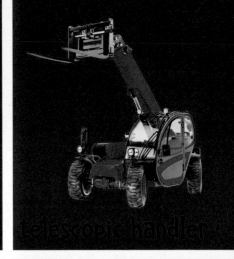

telescopic handler

skid-steer loader

backhoe loader

forklift